Burning Desire

Pleasure Explores Explicit Euthanasia, Embryology,

Sacred Romance

Lana Kendra

it wasn't bought for your personal use only, go back to your favorite ebook retailer and buy your copy. Thank you for acknowledging this author's efforts.

Table of Contents

Content Warning

Due to its sexual content, this book is only for those over the age of legal adulthood. There are some topics with a lot of foul language. All of the characters are at least eighteen years old.

Introduction

Are you in search of an exciting and thrilling book to read? Look no further than this extensive collection of Erotic Suspense book. I offer a wide range of genres, including Romantic Erotica, Fantasy, and Urban BDSM Fiction, to cater to even the most discerning reader. Whether you enjoy Anthologies, Westerns, or Paranormal Romance, I have something to suit your taste. My collection also includes Poetic Folklore, Interracial, Black & African American Literary Criticism, and Gothic Horror for those who crave a deeper and darker reading experience. If you're interested in Futuristic, LGBTQ+, Short Stories, or Lesbian literature, my diverse range of options will keep you captivated. Additionally, I offer Humorous, Victorian, New Adult, and College Women's Psychological Mysteries for those seeking a lighter but equally engaging read. Furthermore, My Fairy Tale Collections,

Transgender, Contemporary Western, Bisexual, and Poetry genres will transport you to different worlds and explore a variety of themes. For my Teen and Young Adult readers, I have a selection of European Geography, Cultures, eBooks, Loners, Outcasts, Mythology, Folk Tales, and much more. With such a wide array of options to choose from, you'll never run out of thrilling and enchanting stories to immerse yourself in.

It is important to emphasize that this content is exclusively intended for individuals who are 18 years of age or older.

Burning Desire

When Atara noticed the big intercity bus approaching from around the corner, she exhaled with relief. Even though she had enjoyed herself immensely at her friend Menucha's wedding, it was past midnight, and all she wanted was to get home and get some rest before having to report to work the next day. Her residence in a city an hour's drive away and the fact that the prior bus was packed didn't help either.

After standing all night in the reception, Atara's legs felt heavy and exhausted as she boarded the bus. Her body appeared exhausted from dancing continually at the energetic event, not just her legs.

With the hopes that this voyage would be more comfortable than the previous one, she moved to the rear seat. "At least the bus is empty," she thought to herself. She could not stand it when some random person kept yapping on a phone and kept her from falling asleep.

A youthful man ran up as the bus departed. He was seated a few rows ahead of Atara when the driver let him in.

Atara recognized Meir, a twenty-three-year-old Yeshiva student with short dark hair and piercing eyes. She recognized him from the wedding earlier in the evening.

Atara ignored him at first, concentrating on her search for a cozy sleeping position. Still, she couldn't get rid of the sensation that there was something fascinating about him. Perhaps it was his remarkable looks or the fact that he was staring out the window, seemingly lost in meditation. Whatever it was, she could not take her eyes off of him.

Atara's mind drifted back to the wedding as the bus rattled along the freeway. Even though her primary reason for attending the party was that Menucha was like a sister to her, she recalled how colorful and wonderful it had been.

Her reverie was interrupted by the sound of Meir's voice.

With his seat shattered, he had shifted closer to her and was now seated almost next her. For a little while, Atara was unsure whether to talk to him or just keep ignoring him. She chose to give him a chance since her curiosity overcame her.

She leaned forward and said, "Hello," breaking the ice.

Surprised by her initiative, Meir looked up. He said, still a little nervous, "Hello." "I didn't expect you to talk to me."

Atara understood his fear and grinned. "Well, I'm bored, and I figured it might be nice to have some company on this long ride."

After that, they started talking more freely and exchanged anecdotes about their lives, careers, and wedding-related events.

"I must say, you looked amazing tonight. It was like you were on fire while dancing. I know I wasn't supposed to look, but it was hard to miss," Meir remarked after a short while.

Atara chuckled softly. "Oh, well, Menucha is like a sister to me. We grew up together, and I've always been there for her during important moments in her life. I think I spent almost as much time in the bridal suite as the couple, helping her get ready!"

"You certainly have the beauty to be the bride," Meir said, his eyes resting on her face.

Atara blushed a little, her heart warmed by the compliment. She was confident that her outfit, which beautifully highlighted her curves, made her look excellent tonight. She boldly pushed forward in her seat so that Meir could see more of her chest. She teased, "Is it my dress, how do you like it?" in her voice.

Meir took a time to gather his thoughts before speaking. His cheeks flushed as he finally said, "It's... stunning." "The color really brings out your eyes, and the fit shows off your figure quite nicely."

Feeling satisfied with his answer, Atara grinned. "I appreciate it," she remarked with increased assurance.

Meir extended her hand and ran it along her thigh, delicately stroking the fabric of her garment. His fingers massaged her, and Atara couldn't help but feel a thrill go through her body. Her breath caught in her throat and her heart raced at the sensation of his electric touch.

They could no longer resist the impulse as a desire-charged atmosphere developed between them. With a passionate kiss, their tongues hungrily explored one other's mouths.

As their kiss intensified, Atara's hands moved over Meir's body, exploring the lines of his well-defined physique beneath his attire. She couldn't believe this stranger had turned her on so much, but she also couldn't ignore their strong bond.

Meir's hands, meantime, tightened around Atara's hips, drawing her into him.

Their breaths mixed in hot, passionate gasps as their kisses grew more intense. Meir's touches became bolder as their excitement intensified, running down Atara's body and caressing her skin through her clothes.

They were unaware of the outer world from the back of the empty bus.

With a quiet sigh, Atara's fingers tangled in his hair. She was giving in to the intense hug, losing her sense of self. Her body cried out for him, aching to be caressed.

Atara said, "It's my stop," gasping for air. "My aprtment is empty, come with me" .

The early morning air slapped them both in the face as they got off the bus. Frantically, they made their way into a neighboring alleyway, Atara tugging at his body so she could force his lips into hers. Being so close to her made her skin feel warm, and he sensed the electricity between them.

As though they were the only two people in the world, the alleyway appeared to be stuck in time. Gently, he ran his hands over her body, stroking her back. She took a step forward him and her breathing became more rapid. He felt shivers run up his spine as she stroked her fingers through his hair and along his neck.

With almost too much intensity, he kissed her tenderly on the lips. Their desire intensified with each kiss, and before long, neither of them was able to contain their feelings. They couldn't stop themselves, not even if they wanted to, and clung to each other like two magnets drawn to each other.

Her lovely breasts were exposed when she removed her top and bra, and he couldn't help but ogle them before exploring more of her body with his hands and lips. He kissed all over the peaks of her nipples in little circles before taking each one in turn, nibbling and sucking. His hands moved down her body, grazing her waist and hips until they eventually came to rest between her legs.

He found her clitoris by licking up from her inner thigh, and he started massaging it with his tongue to elicit the pleasure she had been depriving herself of far too long. Waves of ecstasy washed over her, making her body shake back and forth as his fingers dug deeper into her. He was still hitting her private parts, and she was holding on to his hair tight.

They eventually separated, panting for air, after what seemed like an age. When she saw how visible their location was, she seized his hand and dragged him in the direction of a nearby door. They stumbled into her apartment, pawing at each other on the couch as she opened the door behind them.

Their brains were overtaken by the intense hunger they had, and they couldn't get enough of each other. Meir's touch caused Atara's body to shiver, as his hands expertly cupped her breasts, causing her back to arch with each stroke.

He reached down and cupped her firm ass, then pushed his fingers between her legs to feel more of her wetness.

She gave a sharp cry when he rubbed her clit with his thumb. He touched her, and her body writhed, aching to be freed. He inserted two fingers into her, observing her countenance and seeing her eyes roll back in bliss. He started to stab his fingers in and out, rhythmically pressing his thumb against her clit.

Atara's body shook with every movement as she was swamped with sensations. She encircled him with her arms, keeping him close as he drew her closer to the brink. Her body was aching for more as her breath came out in short, ragged gasps.

Meir quickened the tempo, applying more pressure to her clit and inserting his fingers further into her. With her body bucking furiously and her groans became more intense, Atara let out a loud cry and threw back her head, drawing him nearer with her arms wrapped around his neck.

He kept caressing her, instinctively understanding just how to make her writhe in delight. Tightening her grip on his shoulders, she pressed her nails into his flesh, desperate to cling to the rush of exhilaration that enveloped her.

As she reached her peak, her hips bucked against his palm, causing her body to tremble fiercely. Her orgasm came over her like a tidal wave as she yelled out his name. He kept petting her, seeing the joy on her face as it twisted and turned, till at last she fell back into the couch, content and exhausted.

She curled into his embrace as he came to lie next to her

and ran his fingers through her hair. Their bodies were still buzzing from the after effects of their passion, leaving them both tired.

"That was amazing," Meir said, his voice raspy from longing. "I never expected something like this to happen."

Excited, Atara buried her head in his shoulder, her cheeks reddened. She said, "Neither did I," as she opened her mouth. "But I'm glad it did."

For a few while, they lay close to one another in silence, relishing the intimacy they had just shared.

Idly tracing patterns across Meir's chest, Atara's fingers relished the sensation of his soft flesh under hers. Relishing the sensation of her body against his, he held her tight.

Encouraged by their growing bond, Atara made the decision to go beyond. She turned to face Meir, rolling onto her side, and nipped his lower lip in jest. She stopped and let her words linger in the air, saying, "Now that we're here, and we've already gone this far..." She was shocked by the size and heat of Meir's erect penis as she cautiously reached down and gently grabbed it. Although she had never done something like before, she was motivated to pick up new skills.

She studied the curves and contours of his manhood as her hands slowly circled around it. He felt the chill of her touch on his back and he let out an uncontrollable sigh of pleasure. His desire was further increased by the delicious friction her tender fingers created as they moved smoothly down the length of his penis.

She moved her mouth to his firm member and gently positioned herself on top of him, her breasts pressed on his chest.

She took him in her mouth with determination, felt his shaft lengthen and become harder in return. She moved with purpose and gentleness, creating a seductive rhythm that delighted them both with her tongue and fingers. In the meantime, her own body trembled with expectation as her desire for his touch intensified.

Meir grabbed her by the waist and pulled her closer as she teased him with her tongue and lips. He felt his mouth closing over him, and her quiet moans of pleasure sent chills down his spine.

She sucked him deeper into her mouth, swishing her tongue around the tip, her head nodding rhythmically. She pursed her lips and pursed them again, sending chills down his spine. He gave another moan as her tongue skittered over the tender underside of his shaft.

She carried on with her seductive dance, switching between small caresses and soft suction. Meir groaned softly and thrust his hips forward reflexively as she slid her hand to cup his testicles.

In response, Atara pulled him closer to her lips, opening her lips to take in his entire length. Her fingers kept caressing his balls, exerting precisely the proper amount of pressure to send shivers down his spine.

Meir felt himself drawing nearer to the brink as she ran her mouth up and down his shaft, her lips lightly brushing against his tender flesh. He didn't want to let her down, even though he knew he couldn't hold out much longer.

Sensing the climax he was about to experience, Atara intensified her efforts, her tongue twirling hypnotically around the tip of his penis. Her lips tightened around him, her neck moving in perfect unison with her actions. When she heard his breath stop in his throat, she knew she was doing okay.

Meir's fingers dug into her scalp, tightening their hold on her hair as her tongue and lips synchronized. The first wave of pleasure washed over him, and he tensed up in an attempt to hold back.

Atara pulled him from her mouth just as he was about to lose control, letting him come freely. His essence filled her mouth with his seed, and he groaned deep and primal. With her eyes fixed on his, Atara eagerly swallowed, enjoying the taste of him and communicating a common knowledge of the moment they were in.

With their hearts pounding in rhythm, they lay there intertwined in each other's arms. They were both breathless and ecstatic after their recent intimate and passionate exchange. Curling up against Meir's warm chest, Atara felt his powerful arms encircling her in a protective embrace.

They caught their breath as the afterglow descended upon them. With a sheepish smile, Atara expressed a mix of exhilaration and guilt. "I am not sure what has overcome me," she said, gazing up at him with her large, stunning eyes.

Meir grinned back at her, a feeling of joy and success returning. "You are stunning," he said as he ran his hands through her hair. "And you're not afraid to explore your desires."

Atara's cheeks turned crimson as she flushed. With a gentle and sensitive voice, she answered, "I'm not afraid anymore." "I'm only afraid of missing out on something wonderful."

Meir gently moved in to give her a kiss, his lips lingering on hers briefly before he withdrew. With husky yearning in his voice, he continued, "Then let's enjoy this wonderful thing together."

With a pounding heart from excitement, Atara nodded. They got up and walked together, holding hands all the way to the bathroom.

Atara's cheeks turned red as she flushed. She said, "Thank

you," in a delicate and tender voice. "But I'm not sure if I can handle all of this."

With a comforting smile, Meir moved his hands to her hips. "Don't worry, sweetheart. We'll go slow, and I promise to always respect your boundaries."

A mixture of joy and terror filled Atara as she nodded.

They couldn't help but look at each other, their eyes full of need and curiosity as the warm water cascaded down their bodies as they entered the shower.

Atara felt the force of the water cause her body to shake a little, stiffening her nipples.

Meir stepped behind her, his fingertips trailing down to her hips while his hands glided softly along her sides. Her back was flush against his chest as he lifted her up and caressed her ass. Her body curved towards his, aching for closer touch.

Feeling the gentle curves of her body, he stroked his hands

up and down her sides. She gasped as his fingers touched her nipples and retreated against him. Their bodies were now perfectly aligned as he drew her closer.

Atara pivoted and scrutinized his countenance for any indication of remorse or reluctance. But she saw nothing but hunger and yearning, reflections of her own emotions. With a furious and passionate kiss, she reached up and dragged his face down to hers.

Meir's strong physique was caressed by Atara as she traced the curves of his body with her fingers. Meir gave her the same gesture, running his hands over her curves and ogling her skin's softness.

With her hands reaching down, Atara started to lather herself with the soap. With a glance at Meir, she asked him to come along.

He started at her feet and worked his way up, softly washing her body with the soap in his hands. She shivered in expectation as his touch was hard but delicate.

As he proceeded to wash her body, Atara put her arms around his neck and drew him in. Once more, their mouths came into contact, their tongues moving in time to a rhythmic, passionate exchange.

Meir reached down and cupped her ass and squeezed her cheeks, making Atara sigh with pleasure. His fingers found her entrance, which was already slippery with need, and he slid them between her damp folds. He tormented Atara softly, and she whimpered, her body twitching with eagerness.

She held onto his shoulders, trying to keep her balance while her claws dug into his flesh. Her body ached for release as she let out short, sharp intakes of breath. She took hold of Meir's penis and inserted it between her legs, massaging her crotch along the smooth, firm shaft. She started to grind herself against him in a primal dance of ecstasy, rocking her hips back and forth. With her head thrown back in ecstasy, her lips parted and her eyes closed.

Meir's hands found her breasts again, rubbing and caressing them between his palms. Her hips bucked harder against him as he gently pinched her nipples, making her cry out. She started moving more quickly and urgently in an attempt to elicit an orgasm.

She threw back her head and exclaimed, "Fuck, yes!" as ecstasy flooded her system. Her nails made half-moon imprints as her fingers sank into his shoulders. Pushing faster and harder, he matched her untamed energy with his own. Their movements synchronized, their bodies uniting as one.

Meir's hands moved across her body, his touches growing more forceful and envious. His hardness pressed against her entrance as he grabbed her hips and pulled her in closer. His advances were welcomed by Atara, whose body yearned for the full force of his contact.

Abruptly, Atara thrust herself upon his penis. "Fuck me, stinking dammit!" she yelled.

Meir obeyed without thinking, slamming hard blows into her. Atara threw back her head, shrieking in ecstasy as her eyes rolled into the back of her head. Their mutual pleasures threatened to overwhelm them and push them beyond the confines of the little area.

His steps were smooth and elegant as he moved her at a steady pace. She threw her head back with every strong stroke, her eyes squeezing tight. Trying to stay upright, Atara's hands tightened around the shower bar, causing her knuckles to turn white.

She let out loud yells of delight with every strong push. She crushed herself against Meir, her body aching for more as their motions were perfectly synchronized. Her body was inseparably bound to Meir's. Meir gave a harder, deeper thrust in return, their rhythm perfectly timed.

His thrusts caused Atara's pleasurable shouts to reverberate throughout the shower stall, her voice rising and falling in time with them. With an almost violent force, he drove into her, their bodies uniting in a passionate hug.

Atara's body was shaking and shivering, her muscles tensing as her climax drew near. Her body was entirely at the whim of the powerful feelings coursing through her, and her head was empty. Her yells of exhilaration filled the room as she held desperately to him.

Meir kept digging his teeth into her, his cock pulsating with want to let go. Atara's body begged him to fill her, her walls closing in around him.

As Atara experienced the height of her ecstasy, waves of climax swept over her. Her screams reached a crescendo. Her hips thrusting against his, her body quivered and trembled. She gripped him tightly, her nails scraping down his back.

Meir was about to have his own orgasm and was at his breaking point. With one more, strong thrust, he pushed into her, his cock pulsating as he entered her. With a cry of pleasure, Atara's body tensed and released. Her body trembled from the force of their mutual pleasure as she grabbed onto him.

Atara's knees buckled, causing them to fall to the ground while still connected. Their bodies sated and spent, they clung to one another. The proof of their passion washed away as the warm water kept pouring down their bodies.

Meir's arms encircled Atara, holding her close as they gradually regained breath, hearts thumping in time.

"You're amazing," he muttered, his voice full of passion.

She murmured, "That was fucking amazing," with glassy eyes.

They cherished the intimacy they had just shared for a few

more minutes as they hugged one another. They completed washing each other and caressed each other's bodies as they slowly got to their feet.

After removing their clothes, they showered. Sitting on the bed's edge, Atara's mind was racing.

"I should get you a cab back to your Yeshiva" Atara responded, "And I want your number"

Meir gave a nod, and Atara took her phone.

"I would love to go out with you officially" Meir said. "To find out if we're compatible in more ways than just fucking"

You make a valid point, she answered. "And I'd like to see where this goes."

After bringing up her contacts list, Atara entered Meir's details into her phone. She wrote him a message after that.

Meir's cell rang. He examined the message.

"You put your contact name as Hot Lover?" He chuckled.

With a shrug, Atara laughed. "The shoe fits, doesn't it?" settling into his lap and sensing the twitch of his cock in return. Meir kissed her and said, "Wow, you're unsatisfactory." "You're also a vixen. I adore it, too!"

Atara got to her feet and sent him one more kiss. "I will see you soon," Meir said, nodding and giving her a final kiss before letting her go. They were also alerted to the fact that his cab was outside and started gathering his belongings. He was excited to begin the next chapter and knew that the first thing he would do in the morning would be to phone someone to arrange a meeting between him and Atara.

Acknowledgments

The Glory of this book's success goes to God Almighty and my beautiful Family, Fans, Readers & well-wishers, Customers, and Friends for their endless support and encouragement.

About The Author

I've spent nearly a decade penning romantic novels. As a passionate writer of erotica, I craft dark, romantic erotica. Anime Naked Truth Se of Sacred Sexuality: Forbidden Seducing Short Stories of an Erotica Nude Sexy Girl Poster. Alongside Erotic Mystery Fiction, Victorian Erotica Sex, Black & African American Erotica, Euthanasia, Daddy Teaching, Forced Domination, Alpha Monster Cuckold, and BDSM for Adults, there's an Erotic Fiction in Kinky Family. I write dark, sensual romance because I adore the power of darkness and everything that it entails. Romance novels have always been my favorite kind of books, and now I'm writing them. The idea that you will like reading and enjoying my fiction as much as I enjoy pushing the frontiers of sexual pleasure in my writing thrills me more than anything else.